ANANSI

AND THE SEVEN YAM HILLS

REWRITTEN BY ELIZABETH LANE
ILLUSTRATED BY BRUCE MARTIN

One day Anansi the Spider planted some yams.
First he dug some holes in his garden.
Then he dropped in some yam pieces and covered
them with big hills of dirt.

"My, don't those yam hills look fine!" he said.
"I think I'll count them. One, two, three, four, five, six…"

"...seven!" When Anansi said the word seven, a strange thing happened. He shot into the air, flipped over twice, and came down *kerthump* on the ground.

“Hmmm,” said Anansi, brushing himself off. “I must have said a magic word. Maybe I could use it to trick my friends.”
Soon Pig came down the road and saw Anansi sitting in his garden.

Anansi began to moan and groan. “What’s the matter, Anansi?” Pig asked.
“Woe is me!” cried Anansi. “I’ve planted all these yam hills.
Now I can’t count them!”

"You silly spider!" said Pig. "I can count your yam hills! There are one, two, three, four, five, six…"

"…seven!" When Pig said the word seven, a strange thing happened.
He shot into the air, flipped over twice,
and came down *kerthump* on the ground.

Anansi laughed until his sides ached. Soon Monkey came down the road and saw Anansi sitting in his garden.

Anansi began to moan and groan. “What’s the matter, Anansi?” Monkey asked.
“Woe is me!” cried Anansi. “I’ve planted all these yam hills.
Now I can’t count them!”

"You silly spider!" said Monkey. "I can count your yam hills!
There are one, two, three, four, five, six…"

"...seven!" When Monkey said the word seven,
a strange thing happened.
He shot into the air, flipped over twice,
and came down *kerthump* on the ground.
Anansi laughed until his sides ached.

What fun Anansi had that day! He played the same trick on Tiger.

He played the trick on Snake and Rat…

…and Hippo.

They all shot into the air, flipped over twice, and came down *kerthump* on the ground. Anansi laughed until his sides ached.

All this time, Guinea Fowl was watching from behind a persimmon bush. She crept around the fence and came down the road.

When Anansi saw her, he began to moan and groan.
"What's the matter, Anansi?" Guinea Fowl asked.
"Woe is me!" cried Anansi. "I've planted all these yam hills.
Now I can't count them!"

Guinea Fowl hopped onto one of the yam hills. “I can count them,” she said. “There are one, two, three, four, five, six, and the one I’m sitting on.”

“That’s wrong!” Anansi shouted. “Count them again.”

"One, two, three, four, five, six, and the one I'm sitting on," said Guinea Fowl.
"No!" Anansi screamed. "You're not counting them right!"

“Oh?” said Guinea Fowl. “How am I supposed to count them?”
“You’re supposed to say, one, two, three, four, five, six…”

"...SEVEN!" When Anansi said the word seven, a strange thing happened. He shot into the air, flipped over twice, and came down *kerthump* on the ground.

Pig, Monkey, Tiger, Snake, Rat, Hippo, and Guinea Fowl
all laughed until their sides ached.